Scholar and Gypsy

ANITA DESAI

A Phoenix Paperback

Scholar and Gypsy, *Pineapple Cake* and *Pigeons at Daybreak*
first appeared in *Games at Twilight and Other Stories*
published by William Heinemann Ltd, 1978

This edition published in 1996 by Phoenix
a division of Orion Books Ltd
Orion House, 5 Upper St Martin's Lane, London WC2H 9EA

ISBN 1 85799 765 4

Typeset by Deltatype Ltd, Ellesmere Port, Cheshire
Printed in Great Britain by Clays Ltd, St Ives plc

CONTENTS

Scholar and Gypsy

Her first day in Bombay wilted her. If she stepped out of the air-conditioned hotel room, she drooped, her head hung, her eyes glazed, she felt faint. Once she was back in it, she fell across her bed as though she had been struck by calamity, was extinguished, and could barely bring herself to believe that she had, after all, survived. Sweating, it seemed to her that life, energy, hope were all seeping out of her, flowing down a drain, gurgling ironically.

'But you knew it would be hot,' David said, not being able to help a sense of disappointment in her. He had bought himself crisp bush-shirts of madras cotton and open Kolhapur sandals. He was drinking more than was his habit, it was true, but it did not seem to redden and coarsen him as it did her. He looked so right, so fitting on the Bombay streets, striding over the coconut shells and betel-stained papers and the fish scales and lepers' stumps. 'You could hardly come to India and expect it to be cool, Pat.'

'Hot, yes,' she moaned, 'but not – not *killing*. Not so like death. I feel half-dead, David, sometimes *quite* dead.'

'Shall we go and have a gin-and-lime in the bar?'

She tried that, since it seemed to do him so much good. But

the bar in the hotel was so crowded, the people there were so large and vital and forceful in their brilliant clothes and with their metallic voices and their eyes that flashed over her like barbers' shears, cutting and exposing, that she felt crushed rather than revived.

David attracted people like a magnet – with his charm, his nonchalance, his grace, he did it so well, so smoothly, his qualities worked more efficiently than any visiting card system – and they started going to parties. It began to seem to her that this was the chief occupation of people in Bombay – going to parties. She was always on the point of collapse when she arrived at one: the taxi invariably stank, the driver's hair dripped oil, and then the sights and scenes they passed on the streets, the congestion and racket of the varied traffic, the virulent cinema posters, the blazing colours of women's clothing, the profusion of toys and decorations of coloured paper and tinsel, the radios and loudspeakers never turned to less than top volume, and amongst them flower sellers, pilgrims, dancing monkeys and performing bears . . . that there should be such poverty, such disease, such filth, and that out of it boiled so much vitality, such irrepressible life, seemed to her unnatural and sinister – it was as if chaos and evil triumphed over reason and order. Then the parties they went to were all very large ones. The guests all wore brilliant clothes and jewellery, and their eyes and teeth flashed with such primitive lust as they eyed her slim, white-sheathed blonde self, that the sensation of being caught up and crushed, crowded in and choked, sent her into corners where their knees pushed into her, their hands slid over her back, their voices bored into her, so that when she got back to the hotel, on David's arm, she was more like a corpse than an American globe-trotter.

Folding her arms about her, she muttered at the window, 'I never expected them to be so primitive. I thought it would all be modern, up-to-date. Not this – this wild jungle stuff.'

He was pouring himself a night-cap and splashed it in genuine surprise. 'What do you mean? We've only been seeing the modern and up-to-date. These people would be at home at any New York cocktail party –'

'No,' she burst out, hugging herself tightly. 'No, they would *not*. They haven't the polish, the smoothness, the softness. David, they're *not* civilized. They're still a primitive people. When I see their eyes I see how primitive they are. When they touch me, I feel frightened – I feel I'm in danger.'

He looked at her with apprehension. They had drunk till it was too late to eat and now he was hungry, tired. He found her exhausting. He would have liked to sit back comfortably in that air-conditioned cool, to go over the party, to discuss the people they had met, to share his views with her. But she seemed launched in some other direction she was going alone and he did not want to be drawn into her deep wake. 'You're very imaginative tonight,' he said lightly, playing with the bottle-opener and not looking at her. 'Here was I, disappointed at finding them so westernized. I would have liked them a bit more primitive – at least for the sake of my thesis. Now look at the Gidwanis. Did you ever think an Indian wife would be anything like Gidwani's wife – what was her name?'

'Oh, she was terrible, terrible,' Pat whispered, shuddering, as she thought of the vermilion sari tied below the navel, of the uneven chocolate-smooth expanse of belly and the belt of little silver bells around it. She didn't care to remember the dance she had danced with David on the floor of the night-club. She had never even looked at the woman's face, she had kept her eyes lowered and not been able to go any further than that black navel. If that was not primitive, what could David, a sociology student, mean by the word?

It was at the Gidwanis' dinner later that week that she collapsed. She had begun to feel threatened, menaced, the moment they entered that flat. Leaving behind them the betel-stained walls of the elevator shaft, the servant boys asleep on mats in the passage, the cluster of watchmen and chauffeurs playing cards under the unshaded bulb in the lobby, they had stepped onto a black marble floor that glittered like a mirror and reflected the priceless statuary that sailed on its surface like ships of stone. Scarlet and vermilion ixora in pots. Menservants in stiffly starched uniform. Jewels, enamel, brocade and gold. Gidwani with a face like an amiable baboon's, immediately sliding a soft hand across her back. His wife's chocolate pudding belly with the sari slipping suggestively about her hips. Pat shrank and shrank. Her lips felt very dry and she licked and licked them, nervously. She lost David's arm. Her feet in their sandals seemed to swell grotesquely. She sat at the table, her head slanting. She saw David looking at her concernedly. The manservant's stomach pushed against her shoulder as he lowered the dishes for her. The dishes smelt, she wondered of what – oil, was it, or goat's meat? It was not conducive to appetite. Her fork slipped. The table slipped. She had fainted. They were all crying, shoving, crowding. She pushed at them with her hands in panic.

'David, get me out, get me out,' she blubbered, trying to free herself of them.

Later, sitting at the foot of her bed, 'We'd better leave,' he said sadly. Was it Gidwani's wife's belly that saddened him, she wondered. It was not a sight that one could forget, or discard, or deny. 'Delhi's said to be drier,' he said, 'not so humid. It'll be better for you.'

'But your thesis, David?' she wept, repentantly. 'Will you be able to work on it there?'

'I suppose so,' he said gloomily, looking down at her, shrunk into something small on the bed, paler and fainter each day that she spent in the wild jungles of the city of Bombay.

Delhi was drier. It was dry as a skeleton. Yellow sand seethed and stormed, then settled on wood, stone, flesh and skin, brittle and gritty as powdered bone. Trees stood leafless. Red flowers blazed on their black branches, golden and purple ones burgeoned. Beggars drowsed in their shade, stretched unrecognizable limbs at her. I will pull myself together, Pat said, walking determinedly through the piled yellow dust, I must pull myself together. Her body no longer melted, it did not ooze and seep out of her grasp any more. It was dry, she would hold herself upright, she would look into people's eyes when they spoke to her and smile pleasantly – like David, she thought. But the dust inside her sandals made her feet drag. If she no longer melted, she burnt. She felt the heat strike through to her bones. Even her eyes, protected by giant glare glasses, seemed on fire. She thought she would shrivel up like a piece of paper under a magnifying glass held to reflect the sun. Rubbing her fingers together, she made a scraping, papery sound. Her hair was full of sand.

'But you can't let climate get you down, dear,' David said softly, in order to express tenderness that he hardly felt any longer, seeing her suffer so unbeautifully, her feet dusty, her hair stringy, her face thin and appalled. 'Climate isn't *important*, Pat – rise above it, there's so much *else*. Try to concentrate on *that*.' He wanted to help her. It made things so difficult for him if she wouldn't come along but kept drifting off loosely in some other direction, obliging him to drop things and go after her since she seemed so uncontrolled, dangerously so. He couldn't meet people, work on his thesis, do anything. He had never imagined she could be a burden – not the companion and fellow gypsy she had so fairly promised to be. She came of plain, strong farmer stock – she ought to have some of that blood in her, strong, simple and capable. Why wasn't she capable? He held his hand to her temple – it throbbed hard. They sat sipping iced coffee in a very small, very dark restaurant that smelt, somehow, of railway soot.

'I must try,' she said, flatly and without conviction.

That afternoon she went round the antique shops of New Delhi, determined to take an interest in Indian art and culture. She left the shopping arcade after an hour, horror rising in her throat like vomit. She felt pursued by the primitive, the elemental and barbaric, and kept rubbing her fingers together nervously, recalling those great heavy bosoms of bronze and stone, the hips rounded and full as water-pots, the flirtatious little bells on ankles and bellies, the long, sly eyes that curved out of the voluptuous stone faces, not unlike those of the shopkeepers themselves with their sibilant, inviting voices. Then the gods they showed her, named for her, with their flurry of arms, their stamping feet, their blazing, angered eyes and flying locks, all thunder and lightning, revenge and menace. Scraping the papery tips of her fingers together, she hurried through the dust back to the hotel. Back on her bed, she wept into her pillow for the lost home, for apple trees and cows, for red barns and swallows, for icecream sodas and drive-in movies, all that was innocent and sweet and lost, lost, lost.

'I'm just not sophisticated enough for you,' she gulped over the iced lemon tea David brought her. It was the first time she mentioned the disparity in their backgrounds – it had never seemed to matter before. Laying it bare now was like digging the first rift between them, the first division of raw, red clay. It frightened them both. 'I expect you knew about such things – you must have learnt them in college. You know I only went to high school and stayed home after that –'

'Darling,' he said, with genuine pain and tenderness, and could not go on. His taste would not allow him to, or his scruples: the vulgarity appalled him as much as the pain. 'Do take a shower and have a shampoo, Pat. We're going out –'

'No, no, no,' she moaned in anguish, putting away the iced tea and falling onto her pillow.

'But to quite different people this time, Pat. To see a social worker – I mean, Sharma's wife is a social worker. She'll show you something quite different. I know it'll interest you.'

'I couldn't bear it,' she wept, playing with the buttons of her dress like a child.

But they did prove different. The Delhi intellectual was poorer than the Bombay intellectual, for one thing. He lived in a small, airless flat with whitewashed walls and a divan and bits of folk art. He served dinner in cheap, bright ceramic ware. Of course there was the inevitable long-haired intellectual – either journalist or professor – who sat cross-legged on the floor and held forth, abusively, on the crassness of the Americans, to David's delight and Pat's embarrassment. But Sharma's wife was actually a new type, to Pat. She was a genuine social worker, trained, and next morning, having neatly tucked the night before under the divan, she took Pat out to see a milk centre, a crèche, a nursery school, clinics and dispensaries, some housed in cow sheds, others in ruined tombs. Pat saw workers' babies asleep like cocoons in hammocks slung from tin sheds on building sites; she saw children with kohl-rimmed eyes solemnly eating their free lunches out of brass containers, and schools where children wrote painstakingly on wooden boards with reed pens and the teacher sneezed brown snuff sneezes at her. It was different in content. It was the same in effect. Her feet dragged, dustier by the hour. Her hair was like string on her shoulders. When she met David in the evening, at the hotel, he was red from the sun, like a well-ripened tomato, longing to talk, to tell, to ask and question, while she drooped tired, dusty, stringy, dry, trying to revive herself, for his sake, with little sips of some iced drink but feeling quite surely that life was shrivelling up inside her. She never spoke of apple trees or barns, of popcorn or drug stores, but he saw them in her eyes, more remote and faint every day. Her eyes had been so blue, now they were fading, as if the memory, the feel of apple trees and apples were fading from her. He panicked.

'We'd better go to the hills for a while,' he said: he did not want murder on his hands. 'Sharma said June is bad, very bad, in Delhi. He says everyone who can goes to the hills. Well, we can. Let's go, Pat.'

She looked at him dumbly with her fading eyes, and tried to smile. She thought of the way the child at the hospital had smiled after the doctor had finished painting her burns with gentian violet and given her a plastic doll. It had been a cheap, cracked pink plastic doll and the child had smiled at it through the gentian violet, its smile stamped in, or cut out, in that face still taut with pain, as by a machine. Pat had known that face would always be in pain, and the smile would always be cut out as by the machine of charity, mechanically. The plastic doll and the gentian violet had been incidental.

At the airlines office, the man could only find them seats on the plane to Manali, in the Kulu Valley. To Manali they went.

Not, however, by plane, for there were such fierce sand-storms sweeping through Delhi that day that no planes took off, and they went the three hundred miles by bus instead. The sandstorm did not spare the highway or the bus – it tore through the cracked windows and buried passengers and seats under the yellow sand of the Rajasthan desert. The sun burnt up the tin body of the bus till it was a great deal hotter inside than out in the sun. Pat sat stone-still, as though she had been beaten unconscious, groping with her eyes only for a glimpse of a mango grove or an avenue of banyans, instinctively believing she would survive only if she could find and drink in their dark, damp shade. David kept his eyes tightly shut behind his glare glasses. Perspiration poured from under his hair down his face, cutting rivers through the map of dust. The woman in the seat behind his was sick all the way up the low hills to Bilaspur. In front of him a small child wailed without stop while its mother ate peanuts and jovially threw the shells over her shoulder into his lap. The bus crackled with sand, peanut shells and explosive sounds from the protesting engine. There was a stench of diesel oil, of vomit, of perspiration and stale food such as he had never believed could exist – it was so thick. The bus was long past its prime but rattled, roared, shook and vibrated all the way through the desert, the plains, the hills, to Mandi where it stopped for a tea-break in a rest house under some eucalyptus trees in which cicadas trilled hoarsely. Then it plunged, bent on suicide, into the Beas river gorge.

After one look down the vertical cliff-side of slipping, crumbling slate ending in the wild river tearing through the narrow gorge in a torrent of ice-green and white spray, David's head fell back against the seat, lolled there loosely, and he muttered. 'This is the end, Pat, my girl, I'm afraid it's the end.'

'But it's cooler,' fluted a youthful voice in a rising inflection, and David's head jerked with foolish surprise. Who had spoken? He turned to his wife and found her leaning out of the window, her strings of hair flying back at him in the breeze. She turned to him her excited face – dust-grimed and wan but with its eyes alive and observant. 'I can feel the spray – *cold* spray, David. It's better than a shower or air-conditioning or even a drink. Do just feel it.'

But he was too baffled and stunned and slain to feel anything at all. He sat slumped, not daring to watch the bus take the curves of that precarious path hewn through cliffs of slate, poised above the river that hurtled and roared over the black rocks and dashed itself against the mountainside. He was not certain what exactly would happen – whether the overhanging slate would come crashing down upon them, burying them alive, or if they would lurch headlong into the Beas and be dashed to bits on the rocks – but he had no doubt that it would be one or the other. In the face of this certainty, Pat's untimely revival seemed no more than a pathetic footnote.

To Pat, being fanned to life by that spray-spotted breeze, no such possibility occurred. She was watching the white spray rise and spin over the ice-green river and break upon the gleaming rocks, looking out for small sandy coves where pink oleanders bloomed and banana trees hung their limp green flags, exclaiming with delight at the small birds that skimmed the river like foam – feeling curiosity, pleasure and amusement stir in her for the first time since she had landed in India. She no longer heard the retching of the woman behind them or the faint mewing of the exhausted child in front. Peanut shells slipped into her shoes and out of them. The stench of fifty perspiring passengers was lost in the freshness of the mountains. Up on the ridge, if she craned her neck, she could see the bunched needles of pine trees flashing.

When they emerged from the gorge into the sunlight, apricot-warm and mild, of the Kulu valley, she sat back with a contented sigh and let the bus carry them alongside the now calm and wide river Beas, through orchards in which little apples knobbled the trees, past flocks of royal mountain goats and their blanketed shepherds striding ahead, with the mountaineer's swing, up into the hills of Manali, its deodar forests indigo in the evening air and the snow-streaked rocks of the Rohtang Pass hovering above them, an incredible distance away.

Then they were disgorged, broken sandals, shells, hair, rags, children and food containers, into the Manali bazaar, and the bus conductor swung himself onto the roof of the bus and hurled down their bags and boxes. David was on his knees, picking up the pieces of his broken suitcase and holding them together. The crying child was fed hot fritters his father had fetched from a wayside food stall. The vomiting woman squatted, holding her head in her hands, and a *pai* dog sniffed at her in curiosity and consolation. A big handsome man with a pigtail and a long turquoise earring came up to Pat with an armful of red puppies, his teeth flashing in a cajoling smile. 'Fifty *rupees*,' he murmured, and raised it to 'Eighty' as soon as Pat reached out to fondle the smallest of them. Touts and pimps, ubiquitously small and greasy, piped around David 'Moonlight Hotel, plumbing and flush toilet,' and 'Hotel Paradise, non-vegetarian and best view, sir.'

David, holding his suitcase in his arms, looked over the top of their heads and at the mountain peaks, as if for succour. Then his face tilted down at them palely and he shook his head, his eyes quite empty. 'Let's go, Pat,' he sighed, and she followed him up through the bazaar for he had, of course, made bookings and they had rooms at what had been described to them as an 'English boarding house.'

It was on the hillside, set in a sea of apple trees, and they had to walk through the bazaar to it, nudging past puppy-sellers, women who had spread amber and coral and bronze prayer bells on the pavement, stalls in which huge pans of milk boiled and steamed and fritters jumped up and hissed, and holiday crowds that stood about eating, talking and eyeing the newcomers.

'Jesus,' David said in alarm, 'the place is full of hippies.'

Pat looked at the faces they passed then and saw that the crowd outside the baker's was indeed one of fair men and women, even if they seemed to be beggars. Some were dressed like Indian gurus, in loincloths or saffron robes, with beads around their necks, others as gypsies in pantaloons or spangled skirts, some in plain rags and tatters. All were barefoot and had packs on their backs, and one or two had silent, stupefied babies astride their hips. 'Why,' she said, watching one woman with a child approach an Indian couple with her empty hand out-stretched, 'they might be Americans!' David shuddered and turned up a dusty path that went between the deodar trees to the red-roofed building of the boarding house. But several hippies were climbing the same path, not to the boarding house but vanishing into the forest, or crossing the wooden bridge over the river into the meadows beyond.

14 Americans, Europeans, here in Manali, at the end of the

world – what were they doing? she wondered. Well, what was *she* doing? Ah, she'd come to try and live again. She threw back her shoulders and took in lungfuls of the clear, cold air and it washed through her like water, cleansing and pure. Someone in a red cap was sawing wood outside the boarding house, she saw, and blue smoke curled out of its chimney as in a Grandma Moses painting. There was a sound of a rushing stream below. A cuckoo called. Above the tips of the immense deodars the sky was a clear turquoise, an evening colour, without heat although still distilled with sunlight. Dog roses bloomed open and white on the hillside. She tried to clasp David's arm with joy but he was holding onto the suitcase which had broken its locks and burst open and he could not spare her a finger.

'But David,' she coaxed, 'it's going to be lovely.'

'I'm glad,' he said, white-lipped, and pitched the suitcase onto the wooden veranda at the feet of the proprietor who sat benignly as a Buddha on a wooden upright chair, in a white pullover and string cap, gazing down at them with an expression of pity under his bland welcome.

The room was clean, although bare but for two white iron bedsteads and a dressing table with a small yellow mirror. Its window overlooked a yard in which brown hens pecked and climbed onto overturned buckets and wood piles, and wild daisies bloomed, as white and yellow as fresh bread and butter, around a water pump. The bathroom had no tub but a very well-polished brass bucket, a green plastic mug and, holy of holies, a flush toilet that 15 worked, however reluctantly and complainingly. The proprietor, apple-cheeked and woolly – was he an Anglo-Indian, European or Indian? Pat could not tell – sent them tea and Glaxo biscuits on a tin tray. They sat on the bed and drank the black, bitter tea, sighing 'Well, it's *hot*.'

But Pat could not stay still. Once she had examined the drawers of the dressing table and read scraps from the old newspaper with which they were lined, turned on the taps in the bathroom and washed, changed into her Delhi slippers and drunk her tea, she wanted to go out and 'Explore!' David looked longingly at the clean white, although thin and darned, sheets stretched on the beds and the hairy brown blanket so competently tucked in, but she was adamant.

'We can't waste a minute,' she said urgently, for some unknown reason. 'We mustn't waste this lovely evening.'

He did not see how it would be wasted if they were to lie down on their clean beds, wait for hot water to be brought for their baths and then sleep, but realized it would be somehow craven and feeble for him to say so when she stood at the window with something strong and active in the swing of her hips and a fervour in her newly pink and washed face that he had almost forgotten was once her natural expression – in a different era, a different land.

'We're surrounded by apple trees,' she enticed him, 'and I think, I *think* I heard a cuckoo.'

'Why not?' he grumbled, and followed her out onto the

wooden veranda where the proprietor continued to look

comfortable on that upright chair, and down the garden path to the road that took them into the forest.

It was a deodar forest. The trees were so immensely old and tall that while the lower boughs already dipped their feet into the evening, the tops still brushed the late sunlight, and woolly yellow beams slanted through the black trunks as through the pillars of a shadowy cathedral. The turf was soft and uneven under their feet, wild iris bloomed in clumps and ferns surrounded rocks that were conspicuously stranded here and there. Pat fell upon the wild strawberries that grew with a careless luxuriance – small, seed-ridden ones she found sweet. The few people they passed, village men and women wrapped in white Kulu blankets with handsome stripes, had faces that were brown and russet, calm and pleasant, although they neither smiled nor greeted Pat and David, merely observed them in passing. Pat liked them for that – for not whining or wheedling or begging or sneering as the crowds in Bombay and Delhi had done – but simply conferring on them a status not unlike their own. 'Such independence,' she glowed, 'so self-contained. True mountain people, you know.'

David looked at her a little fearfully, not having noted such a surge of Vermont pride in his country wife before. 'Do you feel one of them yourself?' he asked, a little tentatively.

He was startled by the positive quality of the laugh that rang out of her, by the way she threw out her arms in an open embrace. 'Why, *sure*,' she cried, explosively, and 17 sprang over a small stream that ran over the moss like a trickle of mercury. 'Look, here's dear old Jack in the pulpit,' she cried, darting at some ferns from which protruded that rather sinister gentleman, striped and hooded, David thought, like a silent cobra. She plucked it and strode on, her hair no longer like string but like drawn toffee, now catching fire in the sunbeams, now darkening in the shade. After a while, she remarked 'It isn't much like the friendly Vermont woods, really. It's more like a grand medieval cathedral, isn't it?'

'An observation several before you have made on forests,' he remarked, a trifle drily. 'Is one permitted to sit in your cathedral or can one only kneel?' he asked, lowering himself onto a rock. 'Jesus, is my bottom sore from that bus ride.'

She laughed, threw the Jack in the pulpit into his lap and flung herself on the grass at his feet. And so they might have stopped and talked and laughed a bit before going back to an English supper and their fresh, clean beds but, swinging homewards hand-in-hand, they came suddenly upon a strange edifice on a slope in the forest, like a great pagoda built of wood, heavy and dark timber, rough-hewn and sculpted as a stone temple might be, with trees rearing about it in the twilight, shaggy and dark, like Himalayan bears.

'Could it be a temple?' Pat wondered, for the temples she had so far seen had been bursting at the seams with loud pilgrims and busy beggars and priests, affairs of garish paint and plaster, clatter of bells and malodorous marigolds. A still temple in a silent forest – she had quite lost hope of finding such a thing in this overpopulated land.

'We might go in,' David said since she was straining at his hand and, after hovering at the threshold for a bit, they slipped off their sandals and crossed its high wooden plinth.

It was very much darker inside, like a cave scooped out of a tree trunk. The floor, however, was of clay, hard-packed and silky. A shelf of rock projected from the dark wall and a lamp hung from it with a few flowers bright around its wick. It had that minute been blown out by a tall woman with an appropriately wooden face who wore her hair in a tight plait around her head. She lifted her hand, swung only once but vigorously a large bell, and left with a quick stride, barely glancing at them as she went. They bent to study the stone slab beneath the gently smoking lamp and could only just make out the outline of a giant footprint on it. That was all by way of an image and there were neither offerings nor money-box, neither priest nor pilgrim around.

They came out in silence and walked away slowly, as though afraid something would jump out at them from it, or from the forest – they were so much a part of each other, that forest and its temple.

Finally they emerged from the trees and were within sight of the red roof and chimney pot of the English boarding house amongst its apple trees, far below the snow-streaked black ridges of the mountain pass, still pale and luminous against the darkening sky, at once threatening and protective in its attitude, like an Indian god.

'I'm sure I've never seen anything like that before,' Pat murmured then.

'What, not even in Vermont?' he teased, but received no answer.

They ate their dinner in silence, Pat hugely although reflectively, while David sipped a cup of soup and felt as peevish as a neglected invalid.

Perhaps it was only the smallness of Manali – barely a town, merely an overgrown village, a place for shepherds to halt on their way up to the Pass and over it to Lahaul, and apple growers to load their fruit onto lorries bound for the plains, suddenly struck and swollen by a seasonal avalanche of tourists and their vehicles – that led Pat so quickly to know it and feel it as home. It presented no difficulty, as other Indian towns of her acquaintance had, it was innocent and open and if it did not clamorously and cravenly invite, it did not shut its doors either – it had none to shut. It lay in the cup of the valley, the river and forest to one side, bright paddy fields and apple orchards to the other, open and sunlit, small and easy.

She bought herself a cloth bag to sling over her shoulder and with it strode down the single street of Manali in her friendlily squeaking sandals. She stopped at the baker's for ginger biscuits and to smile, somewhat tentatively, at the hippies who stood barefoot at the door, begging for loaves of bread from Indian tourists who seemed as embarrassed as stupefied to discover that it was not only Indians who could beg, and always gave them far more than they did to poorer Indian beggars. She eyed the vegetable stalls and the baskets of ripe fruit on the pavements with envy, wishing she could set up house and do her own marketing. This walk through the bazaar invariably took her to the Tibetan quarter, a smelly lane that took off to one side. Pat could not explain why she had to visit it daily. David refused to accompany her after one visit. He could not face the open drain that one had to jump over in order to enter one of its slopes. He could not face the yellow *pai* dogs and the abjectly filthy children one had to pass, nor the extraordinary odour of the shops in which sweaty castaway woollens discarded by returning mountaineers and impecunious hippies made soft furry mountains along with Tibetan rugs, exquisitely chased silver candlesticks and bronze icons that democratically lived together with tawdry plastic and glass jewellery, all presided over by stolid women with faces carved intricately out of hard wood. So David thought them. To Pat they were wise and inscrutable old ladies who parted with objects of great value at pathetically low prices. Pushing through old dresses and woollen pullovers that hung from the rafters, she knelt on worn rugs and shuffled through the baubles and beads in order to pick out a lama carved in wood with the elegance of extreme simplicity, bits of turquoise, a ball of amber like solidified honey, a string of prayer beads as cool as river pebbles between her fingers . . .

'Junk, junk, junk,' David groaned as she spread them out on the bed for him to see. 'Couldn't you walk in some other direction? Must it be that bloody bazaar every day?'

'It isn't,' she protested. 'I walk all over. Just come with me and I'll show you,' she offered, but rather indifferently, and he saw that she did not care at all if he came with her or not, while in Bombay or Delhi she would have cared passionately. This needled him into closing his typewriter, laying his papers in the dressing table drawer and coming with her for once, stepping gingerly over the goat droppings and puddles in the yard, out onto the dusty road.

He found she did know, as she had claimed to, every path and stream and orchard in the place for miles, and was determined to prove it to him. To his horror, she even waved and beamed at the drug-struck, meditative hippies as they swung past the Happy Café where they invariably gathered to eat, talk, play on flutes and gaze into space in that dim, dusty interior where a chart hung on the wall offering the *table d'hôte*: daily it was Brown Rice, Beans and Custard. What hippy had carried his macroculture to Manali, David wondered, pinning it to the wall above the counter where flies circled plates of yellow sweetmeats and Britannia Biscuit packets? The faces of the pale Europeans who gathered there seemed to him distressingly vacant, their postures defeated and vague, but when he mentioned this to Pat, she was scornful.

'You're just making up your mind about them without really looking,' she claimed. 'Now look at that man in white robes – doesn't he look like Christ? And it isn't just the bone structure. And see that young man who's always laughing? That's his pet loris on his shoulder. There's another I see in that bazaar sometimes, who has a pet eagle, but he lives way off in the mountains. It's true they don't talk much – but you often see them laugh. Or else they just sit and think. Isn't that beautiful, to be able to do that? I think it's beautiful.'

'I think they're stoned,' he said, happy to leave the Happy Café to its shadowy, macrocultural bliss and climb the steep hill into the deodar forest. 'Lord, must we go to the temple *again*?' he moaned, as she led him forward, having already seen it till he could no longer keep his yawns from cracking his jaws apart while he had again to sit outside, on some excruciating roots, and wait for his wife to pay it a ritual visit. He was not really sure what she did in there, nor did he wish to know. Surely she didn't pray? No, she came out looking much too jolly for that.

But no, today she was taking him for a walk and for a walk she would take him, she said, with that new positivism in her jaw-line and swing of her arms that he rather feared. She led him along a stream in which a man and a woman in gypsy dress – and bald patch, and red curls, respectively – were scrubbing some incredibly blackened pots and pans, like children at play – 'Aren't they charming?' Pat enquired, as if of a painted landscape tastefully peopled with just a few rural figures, and David retorted 'Damn vagabonds' – and down lanes that wound through orchards overhung with apricot trees from which fruit dropped ripe and soft 23 onto the stones under their feet, past farm houses screened by daisies and day lilies from which issued bursts, sometimes of tubercular coughing and sometimes of abstract, atonal music, both curiously foreign, and then uphill, beside a stream that leaped over the rocks like a startled hare, white and flashing between ferns and boulders, to a village of large, square stone and wood houses – the ground floors smaller, built solidly of square blocks of stone, the upper floors larger, their elaborately carved wooden balconies overhanging the courtyards in which cows ate the apricots swept up in hills for them, and children climbed crackling haystacks. Apricot trees festooned with unhealthy-looking mistletoe shaded that village and Pat stopped to ask an old man in a blue cap if he had some to sell. They waited in his courtyard, amongst dung pats and milk pails, standing close to the stone wall to let a herd of mountain goats go by, silk-shawled, tip-tapping and bleat-voiced as a party of tipsy ladies, while the man climbed his tree and plucked them a capful. Eating them out of their pockets – they proved not quite ripe and not as sweet as those sold in the bazaar, but Pat wouldn't say so and David did – they continued uphill, out of the village (David glimpsed a lissom brunette in purple robes and Biblical sandals climbing down to the stream but averted his eyes) into the deodar forest again. David was so grateful for its blue shade, and so overfull with bucolic scenes and apricots, that he was ready to sprawl. His wife sprang on ahead, calling, and then he saw her destination. Another temple. He might have known.

Catching up with her, he found Pat fondling the ears of a big tawny dog that had come barking out of the temple courtyard, with familiarity and a wag of its royal tail. 'We can't go in, it's shut,' she reassured him, 'but do see,' she coaxed, and led him through the courtyard and eventually he had to admit that even as Kulu temples went, this one in Nasogi was a pearl. It was no larger than Hansel and Gretel's hut, its roof sloping steeply to the ground, edged with carved icicles of wood. Its doors and beams were massive, but every bit was elegantly carved and fitted. There was a paved courtyard opening into others, all open and inviting, possibly for pilgrims, and around it a grandeur of trees. David lowered himself onto a root, put his arms around his knees, tilted his head to one side and said 'Well yes, you have something here, Pat, I'll give that to you.'

She glowed. 'I think it's most magical spot on earth, if you'd like to know.'

'Aren't you funny?' he commented. 'I take you the length and breadth of India, I show you palaces and museums, jewels and tiger skins – and all the time you were hankering after a forest and an orchard and a village. Little Gretchen you, little Martha, hmm?'

'Do you think that's all I see in it?' she enquired, and he did not quite like, quite trust her sudden gravity that had something too set about it, too extreme, like that of a fanatic. But what was she being so fanatical about – the country life? A mountain idyll? Surely that was obtainable 25 and possible without fanaticism.

She gave only a hint – it was obvious she had thought nothing out yet, however much she had felt. 'This isn't like the rest of India, Dave. It's come to me as a relief, as an escape from India. You know, down in those horrible cities, I'd gotten to think of India as one horrible temple, bursting, *crawling* with people – people on their knees, *hopeless* people and those horrible idols towering over them with their hundred legs and hundred heads – all *horrible . . .*' (David, tiring of that one adjective, clicked his tongue like an impatient pedagogue, making her veer, only slightly, then return to her track, sifting dry deodar needles through nervous brown fingers) . . . 'and then, to walk through the forest and come upon this – this little shrine – it's like escaping from all those Hindu horrors – it's like coming out into the open and breathing naturally again, without fear. That's what I feel here, you know,' she said with a renewed burst of confidence, 'without *fear*. And you can see that's something I share with, or perhaps have just learnt from, the mountain people here. That's what I admire so in them, in the Tibetans. I don't mean the ones down in the bazaar – those are just like the greasy Indian masses, whining and cajoling and sneering – oh, *horrible* – but the ones one sees on the mountain roads. They're upright, they're honest, independent. They have such a strong swing and a stride to their walk – they walk like gods amongst those crawling, cringing masses. And they haven't those furtive Indian faces either – eyes sliding this way and that, expressions showing

and then closing up – *their* faces are all open, and they laugh
and sing. All they have is a black old kettle and a pack of
wood on their backs, rope sandals and a few sheep, but they
laugh and sing and go striding up the mountains like – like
lords. I watch them all the time, I admire them, you know,
and I got to thinking what makes them so different? I
wondered if it was their religion. I feel, being Buddhists,
they're different from the Hindus, and it must be something
in their belief that gives them this – this fearlessness. When I
come to this shrine and sit and think things out quietly, I can
see where they get their strength from, and their joy . . .'

But here he could stand it no longer. 'Pat, Pat,' he cried,
jumping up and striking his sides. 'You're all confused, Pat,
you're so muddled, so hopelessly muddled! My dear,
addled wife, Pat!'

She frowned and squinted, her fist closed on a handful of
needles, ceased to sift them. 'What do you mean?' she
asked, in a tight, closed voice.

'What do I mean? Don't you know? You're sitting
outside a *Hindu* shrine, this is a *Hindu* temple, and you're
making it out to be a source of Buddhist strength and
serenity! Don't you even know that the Kulu Valley has a
Hindu population, and the shrines you see here are Hindu
shrines?' He whooped with laughter, he pulled her to her
feet and dragged her homeward, laughing so much that
every time she opened her mouth to protest, he drowned her
out with his roars of derision. In the end, that laughter gave
him a headache. 27

He tired of his thesis – the notes he had collected while in Bombay and Delhi and the typescript he was now preparing – long before it was done. The whole job had begun to seem totally irrelevant. Ramming the cover onto the little flat Olivetti, he pushed his legs out so that the waste-paper basket went sprawling, and yawned angrily. The cock on the woodpile at the window caught his eye and gave a wicked wink, but David looked away almost without registering it. Where was Pat?

That was the perennial question these days. Pat was never there. What was more, he no longer asked her where she had been when she appeared for meals or to throw herself down on the bed for the night, her feet raw and dirty from walking in sandals, her cloth bag flung onto the floor. (Once he saw a ragged copy of the Dhammapada slip out of it and hastily looked away: the idea of his poor, addled wife poring over ancient Buddhist texts embarrassed him acutely.) He merely eyed her with accusation and with distaste: she was playing a rôle he had not engaged her to play, she was making a fool of herself, she was embarrassing him, she was absolutely outrageous. As she grew browner from the outdoor life and her limbs sturdier from the exercize, it seemed to him she was losing the fragility, the gentleness that he had loved in her, that she was growing into some tough, sharp countrywoman who might very well carry loads, chop wood, haul water and harvest, but was scarcely fit to be his wife – his, David's, the charming and socially graceful young David of Long Island upbringing – and her movements were marked by rough angles that jarred on him, her voice, when she bothered at all to reply to his vague questions, was brusque and abrupt. It was clear there was no meeting-point between them any more – he would have considered it lowering in status to make a move towards her and she clearly had no interest in meeting him halfway, or anywhere.

He had not cared for the answers she had given him when he had first, mistakenly, asked. On coming upon her one morning, while slouching through the bazaar to post a packet of letters, in, of all places, the Happy Café, round-shouldered on a bench, drinking something cloudy out of a thick glass, in the company of those ragged pilgrims with the incongruously fair heads, he had questioned her with some heat.

'Yes, they're friends of mine,' she shrugged, standing with her new stolidity in the centre of the room to which he had insisted on taking her back. 'I could have told you about them earlier if you'd asked. There's no need for you to spy.'

'Don't be ridiculous,' he snapped. 'Spy on *you*?' What for? Why should it interest me what you do with yourself while I'm slogging away in here –'

'Then why ask?' she snapped back.

His curiosity was larger than his distaste in the beginning. Over dinner he asked her the questions he had earlier resolved not to ask and, pleased with the big plateful of food before her, she had talked pleasantly about the Calfornian couple she had taken up with, and told him the story of their erratic and precipitous voyage from the forests of Big Sur to those of the Kulu Valley, via Afghanistan and Nepal, in search of a guru they had indeed found but now discarded in favour of communal life, vegetarianism and *bhang* which seemed to them a smooth and gentle path to earthly nirvana.

'Nirvana on earth!' he snorted. 'That's a contradiction in terms, don't you know?' Then, seeing her nostrils flare dangerously, went on hastily, but no more wisely, 'Is that what you were drinking down there in that joint, Pat?'

She gave a whoop of delight on seeing the pudding – caramel custard – and buried her nose in a plateful with greed. 'Gee, all this walking makes me hungry,' she apologized, 'and sleepy. Jesus, *how* sleepy.' She went straight to bed.

On another and more uncomfortable occasion, he had found her while out taking the air after a particularly dull and boring day at the typewriter, in the park in front of the Moonlight Hotel and Rama's Bakery where the hippies were wont to gather, some even to sleep at night, rolled in their blankets on the grass. One of the Indian gurus who held court there was seated, lotus style, under a sun-dressed lime tree, with an admiring crowd of fair and tattered hippies about him, his wife Pat as cross-legged, as smiling and as tattered as the rest. He was too far away to hear what they were saying but it seemed more as if they were bandying jokes – what jokes could East and West possibly share? – than meditating or discoursing on theology. What particularly anguished him was the sight of the Indian tourists who had made an outer circle around this central core of seekers of nirvana and bliss-through-*bhang*, as if this were one of the sights of the Kulu Valley that they had paid to see. They stood about with incredulous faces, smiling uneasily, exchanging whispered asides with one another, exactly as if they were watching some disquieting although amusing play. There was condescension and, in some cases, pity in their expressions and attitudes that he could not bear to see directed at his fellow fair-heads, much less at his own wife. He turned and almost raced back to the boarding house.

That evening he had tried to question her again but she was tired, vague, merely brushed the hair from her face and murmured 'Yes, that's Guru Dina Nath. He's so sweet – so gay – so –' and went up to bed. He sniffed the air in the room suspiciously. Was it *bhang*? But he wouldn't know what it smelt like if it were. He imagined it would be sweetish and the air in their room was sour, acid. He wrenched the window open, with violence, hoping to wake her. It did not.

The day he gave up questioning her or pursuing her was when she came in, almost prancing, he thought, like some silly mare, burbling. 'Do you remember Nasogi, David? That darling village where we ate apricots? You remember its temple like a little dolls' house? Well, I met some folks who live in a commune right next to it – a big attic over a 31 cow shed actually, but it overlooks the temple and has an orchard all around it, so it's real nice. Edith – she's from Harlem – took me across, and I had coffee with some of them –'

'Sure it was coffee?' he snarled and, turning his back, hurled himself at the typewriter with such frenzy that she could not make herself heard. She sat on her bed, chewing her lip for a while, then got up and went out again. What she had planned to say to him was put away, like an unsuccessful gift.

She kept out of his way after that, and made no further attempts to take him along with her on the way to nirvana. When, at breakfast, he told her, 'It's time I got back to Delhi. I've got more material to research down there and I can't sit here in your valley and contemplate the mountains any more. I plan to book some seats on that plane for Delhi.'

She was shocked, although she made a stout attempt to disguise it, and he was gratified to see this. 'When d'you want to leave?' she asked, spitting a plum seed into her fist.

'Next Monday, I think,' he said.

She said nothing and disappeared for the rest of the day. She was out again before he'd emerged from his bath next morning, and he had to go down to the bus depot by himself, hating every squalid step of the way: the rag market where Tibetans sold stained and soiled imported clothes to avid Indian tourists and played dice in the dust while waiting for customers, the street where snot-gobbed urchins raced and made puppies scream, only just managing to escape from under roaring lorries and stinking buses. He directed looks of fury at the old beggar without a nose or fingers who solicited him for alms and at the pig-tailed Tibetan with one turquoise ear-ring who tried to sell him a mangy pup. 'We're going to get out of here,' he ground out at them through his teeth, and they smiled at him with every encouragement. The booking office was, however, not yet open for business and he was obliged to wait outside the bus depot which was the filthiest spot in the whole bazaar. He stood slouching against a wooden pillar, watching a half-empty bus push through a herd of worriedly bleating sheep and then come up, boiling and steaming, its green-painted, rose-wreathed sides almost falling apart with the effort. It groaned the last few yards of the way and expired at his feet, with a hiss of steam that made its bonnet rise inches into the air.

The driver, a wiry young Sikh who had hung his turban on a peg by the seat and wore only a purple handkerchief over his top-knot, leaped out and raced around to fling open the bonnet before the contraption exploded. His assistant, who had jumped down from the back door and vanished into the nearest shop, a grocer's, now came running out with an enamel jug of water which the driver grabbed from his hands and, before David's incredulous eyes, threw onto the radiator.

The next thing that David knew was that an explosion of steam and boiling water had hit him, hit the driver, the assistant and he didn't know how many bystanders – he couldn't see, he flung his hands to his face, but too late, he was on fire, he was howling – everyone was howling. Someone grabbed his shoulders, someone shouted 'Sir, sir, are you blind? Are you blind?' and he roared 'Yes, damn you, I'm blind, *blind*.' And where was Pat, his bloody useless wife, where was *she*? Here was he, blinded, scalded, being dragged through the streets by strangers, madmen, all trying to carry him, all babbling as at a universal holocaust.

'There, try opening your eyes now. I think you can, son, just try it,' a blessedly American voice spoke, and prised away his hands from his face. In his desperation to see the owner of this blessed voice, David allowed his hands to be loosed from his face and actually opened his eyes – an act he had never thought to perform again – and gazed upon the American doctor with the auburn sideburns and the shirt of blue and brown checked wool as at a vision of St Michael at the golden gates. 'That's wonderful, just wonderful,' beamed the gorgeous man, solid and middle-aged and wondrously square. 'You haven't lost your eyes, see. Now let me just paint those burns for you and you'll leave here as fit as a fidle, see if you don't . . .' So he burbled on, in that rich, heavy voice from the Middle West, and David sat back as helpless as a baby, and felt those large dry hands with their strong growth of ginger hair gently dab at his face, bringing peace and blessing in their wake. He was the American mission hospital doctor but to David he was God himself on an inspection visit mercifully timed to coincide

34

with David's accident.

It was David's accident. He quite forgot to ask about the driver or his brainless help or the hapless bystanders who had been standing too close to the boiling radiator. He merely sat there, limp and helpless, feeliing the doctor's voice flow over him like a stream of American milk. And then he was actually handed a glass of milk – Horlicks, the doctor called it, sweet and hot, and he sipped it with bowed head like a child, afraid he would cry now that the agony was over and the convalescence so sweetly begun.

'It's the shock,' the doctor was saying kindly. 'Your eyes are quite safe, son, and the burns are superficial – luckily – it's just the shock,' and he patted David on the back with those ginger-tufted hands that were so square and sure. 'We see all kinds of accidents up here, you kow. Yesterday it was one of those crazy hippies who had to be brought in on a stretcher. He'd fallen off a mountain. Now can you credit that? A grown man just going and falling off a mountain like he was a kid? He'd broken both legs, see. I had to send my assistant with him to Delhi. They'll have quite a time getting him on his feet again but the Holy Family Hospital tries its best. Still,' he added, in the considerate manner of one who knows how to deal with a patient, 'yours sure is the most *unnecessary* accident we've had, I'll say that,' he declared, filling David with sweet pride. Bowing his head, he sipped his milk and drank in the doctor's kindly gossip. He tried to say 'Yeah, those hippies – they shouldn't be allowed – I don't see how they're allowed –' but his voice

35

died away and the doctor shrugged tolerantly and laughed. 'It takes all kinds, you know, but they really are kids, they shouldn't be allowed out of their mamma's sight. How about another drink of Horlicks? You think you can walk home now? Feel okay, son?' David would have given a great deal to say he was not okay at all, that he couldn't possibly walk home, that he wanted to stay and tell the doctor all about Pat, how she had practically deserted him, and about the unsavoury friends she had made here. He wanted to ask him to speak to Pat, reason with her, return his wife to him, return his former life to him. It made him weep, almost, to think that he was expected to get up and walk out. He threw a look of anguish at the doctor as he was seen down the rickety stairs to the bus depot, and did not realize that no one could make out his expression through that coating of gentian violet that coloured his entire face, neck and ears with an extraordinary neon glow.

'My God, what's up with *you*?' screamed Pat when she came in, hours later, and was struck still by shock.

He glared at her, exulting at having elicited such a response from her. But a minute later he saw that she had collapsed against the door frame, not with shock, but with laughter.

'What have you *done*, Dave?' she squealed. 'What made you do *that*?'

Harsh words were exchanged then. David, having lost his tight-lipped control (that morning's sweet Horlicks had washed it away) demanded roughly where she had been when he was standing in the sun to buy tickets and getting scalded and very nearly blinded in the process. Didn't she care about him, he wanted to know, and what *did* she care about it all now? And she, revolted, she said, by his egoism and conceit that didn't allow him to see beyond the tip of his nose – what was wrong with him that he couldn't move out of the way of a bus, for Christ's sake, didn't it just show that he saw nothing, noticed nothing outside himself? – told him what she cared about. She had found a place for herself in the commune at Nasogi. It was what she was meant for, she realized – not going to parties with David, but to live with other men and women who shared her beliefs. They were going to live the simple life, wash themselves and their dishes in a stream, cook brown rice and lentils, pray and meditate in the forest and, at the end, perhaps, become Buddhists – 'A Buddhist, you crackpot? In a Hindu temple?' he spluttered – but she continued calmly that she was sure to find, in the end, something that could not be found on the cocktail rounds of Delhi, Bombay or even, for that matter, Long Island, but that she was positive existed here, in the forest, on the mountains.

'What cocktail rounds? Are you trying to imply I'm a social gadabout, not a serious student of sociology, working on a thesis on which my entire career is based?'

'Working on a thesis?' she screeched derisively. 'Sociology? The idea of you, Dave, when you've never so much as looked, I mean really looked, into the soul, the *prana*, of the 37 next man – is just too –' she spluttered to a stop, wildly threw her hair about her face and burst out 'You, you don't even know it's possible to find Buddha in a Hindu temple. Why, you can find him in a church, a forest, anywhere. Do you think he's as narrow-minded as *you*?' she slung at him, and the explosiveness with which this burst from her showed how his derision had cut into her, how it had festered in her.

The English boarding house was treated to much more hurling of American abuse that night, to throwing around of suitcases, to sounds of packing and dramatic partings and exits, and many heads leant out of the windows into the chalky moonlight to see Pat set off, striding through the daisy-spattered yard in her newly acquired hippy rags that whipped against her legs a she marched off, bag and prayer beads in hand, with never a backward look. There was no one, however, but the proprietor, bland and inscrutable as ever, to see David off next morning making a quieter, neater and sadder departure for Delhi, unconventional only on account of the brilliant purple hue of his face.

If the truth were to be told, he felt greater regret at having to arrive in Delhi with a face like a painted baboon's than to arrive without his wife.

Pineapple Cake

Victor was a nervous rather than rebellious child. But it made no difference to his mother: she had the same way of dealing with nerves and rebels.

'You like pineapple cake, don't you? Well, come along, get dressed quickly – yes, yes, the velvet shorts – the new shoes, yes – hurry – pineapple cake for good boys. . . .'

So it had gone all afternoon and, by holding out the bait of pineapple cake, his favourite, Mrs Fernandez had the boy dressed in his new frilled shirt and purple velvet shorts and new shoes that bit his toes and had him sitting quietly in church right through the long ceremony. Or so she thought, her faith in pineapple cake being matched only by her faith in Our Lady of Mount Mary, Bandra Hill, Bombay. Looking at Victor, trying hard to keep his loud breathing bottled inside his chest and leaning down to see what made his shoes so vicious, you might have thought she had been successful, but success never satisfies and Mrs Fernandez sighed to think how much easier it would have been if she had had a daughter instead. Little girls love weddings, little girls play at weddings, little girls can be dressed in can-can petticoats and frocks like crêpe-paper bells of pink and orange, their oiled and ringleted hair crowned with rustling wreaths of paper flowers. She glanced around her rather tiredly to hear the church rustling and crepitating with excited little girls, dim and dusty as it was, lit here and there by a blazing afternoon window of red and blue glass, a flare of candles or a silver bell breathless in the turgid air. This reminded her how she had come to this church to pray and light candles to Our Lady when she was expecting Victor, and it made her glance down at him and wonder why he was perspiring so. Yes, the collar of the frilled shirt was a bit tight and the church was airless and stuffy but it wasn't very refined of him to sweat so. Of course all the little boys in her row seemed to be in the same state – each one threatened or bribed into docility, their silence straining in their chests, soundlessly clamouring. Their eyes were the eyes of prisoners, dark and blazing at the ignominy and boredom and injustice of it all. When they shut their eyes and bowed their heads in prayer, it was as if half the candles in church had gone out, and it was darker.

Relenting, Mrs Fernandez whispered, under cover of the sonorous prayer led by the grey padre in faded purple, 'Nearly over now, Victor. In a little while we'll be going to tea – pineapple cake for you.'

Victor hadn't much faith in his mother's promises. They had a way of getting postponed or cancelled on account of some small accidental lapse on his part. He might tear a hole in his sleeve – no pocket money. Or stare a minute too long at Uncle Arthur who was down on a visit from Goa and had a wen on the back of his bald head – no caramel custard for pudding. So he would not exchange looks with her but stared stolidly down at his polished shoes, licked his dry lips and wondered if there would be Fanta or Coca-Cola at tea.

Then the ceremony came to an end. How or why, he could not tell, sunk so far below eye-level in that lake of breathless witnesses to the marriage of Carmen Maria Braganza of Goa and George de Mello of Byculla, Bombay. He had seen nothing of it, only followed, disconsolately and confusedly, the smells and sounds of it, like some underground creature, an infant mole, trying to make out what went on outside its burrow, and whether it was alarming or enticing. Now it was over and his mother was digging him in the ribs, shoving him out, hurrying him by running into his heels, and now they were streaming out with the tide. At the door he made out the purple of the padre's robes, he was handed a pink paper flower by a little girl who held a silver basket full of them and whose face gleamed with fanatic self-importance, and then he was swept down the stairs, held onto by his elbow and, once on ground level, his mother was making a din about finding a vehicle to take them to the reception at Green's. 'The tea will be at Green's, you know,' she had been saying several times a day for weeks now. 'Those de Mellos must have money – they can't be so badly off – tea at Green's, after all.'

It was no easy matter, she found, to be taken care of, for although there was a whole line of cabs at the kerb, they all belonged to the more important members of the de Mello and Braganza families. When Mrs Fernandez realized this, she set the lips together and looked dangerously wrathful, and the party atmosphere began quickly to dissolve in the acid of bad temper and the threat to her dignity. Victor stupidly began a fantasy of slipping out of her hold and breaking into a toy shop for skates and speeding ahead of the whole caravan on a magic pair, to arrive at Green's before the bride, losing his mother on the way . . . But she found two seats, in the nick of time, in a taxi that already contained a short, broad woman in a purple net frock and a long thin man with an adam's apple that struggled to rise above his polka-dotted bow tie and then slipped down again with an audible croak. The four of them sat squeezed together and the women made little remarks about how beautiful Carmen Maria had looked and how the de Mellos couldn't be badly off, tea at Green's, after all. 'Green's', the woman in the purple net frock yelled into a taxi driver's ear and gave her bottom an important shake that knocked Victor against the door. He felt that he was being shoved out, he was not wanted, he had no place here. This must have made him look piqued for his mother squeezed his hand and whispered, 'You've been a good boy – pineapple cake for you.' Victor sat still, not breathing. The man with the adam's apple stretched his neck longer and longer, swivelled his head about on the top of it and said nothing, but the frog in his throat gurgled to itself.

Let out of the taxi. Victor looked about him at the

wonders of Bombay harbour while the elders tried to be polite and yet not pay the taxi. Had his father brought him here on a Sunday outing, with a ferry boat ride and a fresh coconut drink for treats, he would have enjoyed the Arab dhows with their muddy sails, the ships and tankers and seagulls and the Gateway of India like a coloured version of the photograph in his history book, but it was too unexpected. He had been promised pineapple cake at Green's, sufficiently ovewhelming in itself – he hadn't the wherewithal to cope with the Gateway of India as well.

Instinctively he put out his hand to find his mother's and received another shock – she had slipped on a pair of gloves, dreadfully new ones of crackling nylon lace, like fresh bandages on her purple hands. She squeezed his hand, saying 'If you want to do soo-soo, tell me, I'll find the toilet. Don't you go and wet your pants, man.' Horrified, he pulled away but she caught him by the collar and led him into the hotel and up the stairs to the tea room where refreshments were to be served in celebration of Carmen Maria's and George de Mello's wedding. The band was still playing 'Here Comes The Bride' when Victor and his mother entered.

Here there was a repetition of the scene over taxi: this time it was seats at a suitable table that Mrs Fernandez demanded, could not find, then spotted, was turned away from and, finally, led to two others by a slippery-smooth waiter used to such scenes. The tables had been arranged in the form of the letter E, and covered with white cloths. Little vases marched up the centres of the tables, sprouting stiff zinnias and limp periwinkles. The guests, chief and otherwise, seemed flustered by the arrangements, rustled about, making adjustments and readustments, but the staff showed no such hesitations over protocol. They seated the party masterfully, had the tables laid out impeccably and, when the band swung into the 'Do Re Mi' song from *The Sound of Music*, brought in the wedding cake. Everyone craned to see Carmen Maria cut it, and Victor's mother gave him a pinch that made him half-rise from his chair, whispering, 'Stand up if you can't see, man, stand up to see Carmen Maria cut the cake.' There was a burst of laughter, applause and raucous congratulation with an undertone of ribaldry that unnerved Victor and made him sink down on his chair, already a bit sick.

The band was playing a lively version of 'I am Sixteen, Going on Seventeen' when Victor heard a curious sound, as of a choked drain being forced. Others heard it too, for suddenly chairs were being scraped back, people were standing up, some of them stepped backwards and nearly fell on top of Victor who hastily got off his chair. The mother of the bride, in her pink and silver gauzes, ran up, crying 'Oh no, oh no, no, no!'

Two seats down sat the man with the long, thin neck in which an adam's apple rose and fell so lugubriously. Only he was no longer sitting. He was sprawled over his chair, his head hanging over the back in a curiously unhinged way, as though dangling at the end of a rope. The woman in the purple net dress was leaning over him and screaming 'Aub, Aub, my darling Aubrey! Help my darling Aubrey!' Victor gave a shiver and stepped back and back till someone caught and held him.

Someone ran past – perhaps one of those confident young waiters who knew all there was to know – shouting 'Phone for a doctor, quick! Call Dr Patel,' and then there was a long, ripping groan all the way down the tables which seemed to come from the woman in the purple net dress or perhaps from the bride's mother, Victor could not tell – 'Oh, why did it have to happen *today*? Couldn't he have gone into another day?' Carmen Maria, the bride, began to sob frightenedly. After that someone grasped the long-necked old man by his knees and armpits and carried him away, his head and his shoes dangling like stuffed paper bags. The knot of guests around him loosened and came apart to make way for what was obviously a corpse.

Dimly, Victor realized this. The screams and sobs of the party-dressed women underlined it. So did the slow, stunned way in which people rose from the table, scraped back their chairs and retreated to the balcony, shaking their heads and muttering, 'An omen, I tell you, it must be an omen.' Victor made a hesitant move towards the balcony – perhaps he would see the hearse arrive.

But Victor's mother was holding him by the arm and she gave it an excited tug. 'Sit *down*, man,' she whispered furtively, 'here comes the pineapple cake,' and, to his amazement, a plate of pastries was actually on the table now – iced, coloured and gay. 'Take it, take the pineapple cake,' she urged him, pushing him towards the plate, and when the boy didn't move but stared down at the pastry dish as though it were the corpse on the red rexine sofa, her mouth gave an impatient twitch and she reached out to fork the pineapple cake onto her own plate. She ate it quickly. Wiping her mouth primly, she said, 'I think we'd better go now.'

Pigeons at Daybreak

One of his worst afflictions, Mr Basu thought, was not to be able to read the newspapers himself. To have them read to him by his wife. He watched with fiercely controlled irritation that made the corners of his mouth jerk suddenly upwards and outwards, as she searched for her spectacles through the flat. By the time she found them – on the ledge above the bathing place in the bathroom, of all places: what did she want with her spectacles in *there*? – she had lost the newspaper. When she is found it, it was spotted all over with grease for she had left it beside the stove on which the fish was frying. This reminded her to see to the fish before it was overdue. 'You don't want charred fish for your lunch, do you?' she shouted back when he called. He sat back then, in his tall-backed cane chair, folded his hands over his stomach and knew that if he were to open his mouth now, even a slit, it would be to let out a scream of abuse. So he kept it tightly shut.

When she had finally come to the end of that round of bumbling activity, moving from stove to bucket, shelf to table, cupboard to kitchen, she came out on the balcony again, triumphantly carrying with her the newspaper as

47

well as the spectacles. 'So,' she said, 'are you ready to listen to the news now?'

'Now,' he said, parting his lips with the sound of tearing paper, 'I'm ready.'

But Otima Basu never heard such sounds, such ironies or distresses. Quite pleased with all she had accomplished, and at having half an hour in which to sit down comfortably, she settled herself on top of a cane stool like a large soft cushion of white cotton, oiled hair and gold bangles. Humming a little air from the last Hindi film she had seen, she opened out the newspaper on her soft, doughy lap and began to hum out the headlines. In spite of himself, Amul Basu leaned forward, strained his eyes to catch an interesting headline for he simply couldn't believe this was all the papers had to offer.

' "Rice smugglers caught" ' she read out, but immediately ran along a train of thought of her own. 'What can they expect? Everyone knows there is enough rice in the land, it's the hoarders and black-marketeers who keep it from us, naturally people will break the law and take to smuggling . . .'

'What else? What else?' Mr Basu snapped at her. 'Nothing else in the papers?'

'Ah – ah – hmm,' she muttered as her eyes roved up and down the columns, looking very round and glassy behind the steel-rimmed spectacles. ' "Blue bull menace in Delhi airport can be solved by narcotic drug –" '

'Blue bulls? Blue bulls?' snorted Mr Basu, almost tipping

out his chair. 'How do you mean, "blue bulls"? What's a blue bull? You can't be reading right.'

'I am reading right,' she protested. 'Think I can't read? Did my B.A., helped two children through school and college, and you think I can't read? Blue bulls it says here, blue bulls it is.'

'Can't be,' he grumbled, but retreated into his chair from her unexpectedly spirited defence. 'Must be a printing mistake. There are bulls, buffaloes, bullocks, and *bul-buls*, but whoever heared of a blue bull? Nilgai, do they mean? But that creature is nearly extinct. How can there be any at the airport? It's all rot, somebody's fantasy –'

'All right, I'll stop reading, if you'd rather. I have enough to do in the kitchen, you know,' she threatened him, but he pressed his lips together and, with a little stab of his hand, beckoned her to pick up the papers and continue.

'Ah – ah – hmm. What pictures are on this week, I wonder?' she continued, partly because that was a subject of consuming interest to her, and partly because she thought it a safe subject to move onto. '*Teri Meri Kismet* – "the heartwarming saga of an unhappy wife". No, no, no. *Do Dost* – winner of three Filmfare awards – ahh . . .'

'Please, please, Otima, the news,' Mr Basu reminded her.

'Nothing to interest you,' she said but tore herself away from the entertainments column for his sake. 'Anti-arthritis drug' – not your problem. 'Betel leaves cause cancer.' Hmph. I know at least a hundred people who chew betel leaves and are as fit –'

49

'All right. All right. What else?'

'What news are you interested in then?' she flared up, but immediately subsided and browsed on, comfortably scratching the sole of her foot as she did so. ' "Floods in Assam." "Drought in Maharashtra." When is there not? "Two hundred cholera deaths." "A woman and child have a miraculous escape when their house collapses." "Husband held for murder of wife." See?' she cried excitedly. 'Once more. How often does this happen? "Husband and mother-in-law have been arrested on charge of pouring kerosene on Kantibai's clothes and setting her on fire while she slept." Yes, that is how they always do it. Why? Probably the dowry didn't satisfy them, they must have hoped to get one more . . .'

He groaned and sank back in his chair. He knew there was no stopping her now. Except for stories of grotesque births like those of two-headed children or five-legged calves, there was nothing she loved as dearly as tales of murder and atrocity, and short of his having a stroke or the fish-seller arriving at the door, nothing could distract her now. He even heaved himself out of his chair and shuffled off to the other end of the balcony to feed the parrot in its cage a green chilli or two without her so much as noticing his departure. But when she had read to the end of that fascinating item, she ran into another that she read out in a voice like a law-maker's, and he heard it without wishing to: ' "Electricity will be switched off as urgent repairs to

power lines must be made, in Darya Ganj and Kashmere

Gate area, from 8 p.m. to 6 a.m. on the twenty-first of May." My God, that is today.'

'Today? Tonight? No electricity?' he echoed, letting the green chilli fall to the floor of the cage where other offered and refused chillies lay in a rotting heap. 'How will I sleep then?' he gasped fearfully, 'without a fan? In this heat?' and already his diaphragm seemed to cave in, his chest to rise and fall as he panted for breath. Clutching his throat, he groped his way back to the cane chair. 'Otima, Otima, I can't breathe,' he moaned.

She put the papers away and rose with a sigh of irritation and anxiety, the kind a sickly child arouses in its tired mother. She herself, at fifty-six, had not a wrinkle on her oiled face, scarcely a grey hair on her head. As smooth as butter, as round as a cake, life might still have been delectable to her if it had not been for the asthma that afflicted her husband and made him seem, at sixty-one, almost decrepit.

'I'll bring you your inhaler. Don't get worried, just don't get worried,' she told him and bustled off to find his inhaler and cortisone. When she held them out to him, he lowered his head into the inhaler like a dying man at the one straw left. He grasped it with frantic hands, almost clawing her. She shook her head, watching him. 'Why do you let yourself get so upset?' she asked, cursing herself for having read out that particular piece of news to him. 'It won't be so bad. Many people in the city sleep without electric fans – most do. We'll manage –'

'*You'll* manage,' he spat at her, 'but I?'

There was no soothing him now. She knew how rapidly he would advance from imagined breathlessness into the first frightening stage of a full-blown attack of asthma. His chest was already heaving, he imagined there was no oxygen left for him to breathe, that his lungs had collapsed and could not take in any air. He stared up at the strings of washing that hung from end to end of the balcony, the overflow of furniture that cluttered it, the listless parrot in its cage, the view of all the other crowded, washing-hung balconies up and down the length of the road, and felt there was no oxygen left in the air.

'Stay out here on the balcony, it's a little cooler than inside,' his wife said calmly and left him to go about her work. But she did it absently. Normally she would have relished bargaining with the fish-seller who came to the door with a *beckti*, some whiskered black river fish and a little squirming hill of pale pink prawns in his flat basket. But today she made her purchases and paid him off rather quickly – she was in a hurry to return to the balcony. 'All right?' she asked, looking down at her husband sunk into a heap on his chair, shaking with the effort to suck in air. His lips tightened and whitened in silent reply. She sighed and went away to sort out spices in the kitchen, to pour them out of large containers into small containers, to fill those that were empty and empty those that were full, giving everything that came her way a little loving polish with the end of her sari for it was something she loved to do, but she did not stay very long. She worried about her husband. Foolish and unreasonable as he seemed to her in his sickness, she could not quite leave him to his agony, whether real or imagined. When the postman brought them a letter from their son in Bhilai, she read out to him the boy's report on his work in the steel mills. The father said nothing but seemed calmer and she was able, after that, to make him eat a little rice and fish *jhol*, very lightly prepared, just as the doctor prescribed. 'Lie down now,' she said, sucking at a fish bone as she removed the dishes from the table. 'It's too hot out on the balcony. Take some rest.'

'Rest?' he snapped at her, but shuffled off into the bedroom and allowed her to make up his bed with all the pillows and bolsters that kept him in an almost sitting position on the flat wooden bed. He shifted and groaned as she heaped up a bolster here, flattened a cushion there, and said he could not possibly sleep, but she thought he did for she kept an eye on him while she leafed through a heap of film and women's magazines on her side of the bed, and thought his eyes were closed genuinely in sleep and that his breathing was almost as regular as the slow circling of the electric fan above them. The fan needed oiling, it made a disturbing clicking sound with every revolution, but who was there to climb up to it and do the oiling and cleaning? Not so easy to get these things done when one's husband is old and ill, she thought. She yawned. She rolled over.

When she brought him his afternoon tea, she asked 'Had a good sleep?' which annoyed him. 'Never slept at all,' he snapped, taking the cup from her hands and spilling some tea. 'How can one sleep if one can't breathe?' he growled, and she turned away with a little smile at his stubbornness. But later that evening he was genuinely ill, choked, in a panic at his inability to breathe as well as at the prospect of a hot night without a fan. 'What will I do?' he kept moaning in between violent struggles for air that shook his body and left it limp. 'What will I do?'

'I'll tell you,' she suddenly answered, and wiped the perspiration from her face in relief. 'I'll have your bed taken up on the terrace. I can call Bulu from next door to do it – you can sleep out in the open air tonight, eh? That'll be nice, won't it? That will do you good.' She brightened both at the thought of a night spent in the open air on the terrace, just as they had done when they were younger and climbing up and down stairs was nothing to them, and at the thought of having an excuse to visit the neighbours and having a little chat while getting them to come and carry up a string bed for them. Of course old Basu made a protest and a great fuss and coughed and spat and shook and said he could not possibly move in this condition, or be moved by anyone, but she insisted and, ignoring him, went out to make the arrangements.

Basu had not been on the terrace for years. While his wife and Bulu led him up the stairs, hauling him up and propping him upright by their shoulders as though he were some lifeless bag containing something fragile and valuable, he tried to think when he had last attempted or achieved what now seemed a tortuous struggle up the steep concrete steps to the warped green door at the top.

They had given up sleeping there on summer nights long ago, not so much on account of old age or weak knees, really, but because of their perpetual quarrels with the neighbours on the next terrace, separated from theirs by only a broken wooden trellis. Noisy, inconsiderate people, addicted to the radio turned on full blast. At times the man had been drunk and troubled and abused his wife who gave as good as she got. It had been intolerable. Otima had urged her husband, night after night, to protest. When he did, they had almost killed him. At least they would have had they managed to cross over to the Basus' terrace which they were physically prevented from doing by their sons and daughters. The next night they had been even more offensive. Finally the Basus had been forced to give in and retreat down the stairs to sleep in their closed, airless room under the relentlessly ticking ceiling fan. At least it was private there. After the first few restless nights they wondered how they had ever put up with the public sleeping outdoors and its disturbances – the 'nuisance', as Otima called it in English, thinking it an effective word.

That had not – he groaned aloud as they led him up over the last step to the green door – been the last visit he had paid to the rooftop. As Bulu kicked open the door – half-witted he may be, but he was burly too, and good-natured, like so many half-wits – and the city sky revealed itself, in its dirt-swept greys and mauves, on the same level with them,

Basu recalled how, not so many years ago, he had taken his daughter Charu's son by the hand to show him the pigeon roosts on so many of the Darya Ganj rooftops, and pointed out to him a flock of collector's pigeons like so many silk and ivory fans flirting in the sky. The boy had watched in silence, holding onto his grandfather's thumb with tense delight. The memory of it silenced his groans as they lowered him onto the bed they had earlier carried up and spread with his many pillows and bolsters. He sat there, getting back his breath, and thinking of Nikhil. When would he see Nikhil again? What would he not give to have that child hold his thumb again and go for a walk with him!

Punctually at eight o'clock the electricity was switched off, immediately sucking up Darya Ganj into a box of shadows, so that the distant glow of Connaught Place, still lit up, was emphasized. The horizon was illuminated as by a fire, roasted red. The traffic made long stripes of light up and down the streets below them. Lying back, Basu saw the dome of the sky as absolutely impenetrable, shrouded with summer dust, and it seemed to him as airless as the room below. Nikhil, Nikhil, he wept, as though the child might have helped.

Nor could he find any ease, any comfort on that unaccustomed string bed (the wooden pallet in their room was of course too heavy to carry up, even for Bulu). He complained that his heavy body sank into it as into a hammock, that the strings cut into him, that he could not turn on that wobbling net in which he was caught like some dying fish, gasping for air. It was no cooler than it had been indoors, he complained – there was not the slightest breeze, and the dust was stifling.

Otima soon lost the lightheartedness that had come to her with this unaccustomed change of scene. She tired of dragging around the pillows and piling up the bolsters, helping him into a sitting position and then lowering him into a horizontal one, bringing him his medicines, fanning him with a palm leaf and eventually of his groans and sobs as well. Finally she gave up and collapsed onto her own string bed, lying there exhausted and sleepless, too distracted by the sound of traffic to sleep. All through the night her husband moaned and gasped for air. Towards dawn it was so bad that she had to get up and massage his chest. When done long and patiently enough, is seemed to relieve him.

'Now lie down for a while. I'll go and get some iced water for your head,' she said, lowering him onto the bed, and went tiredly down the stairs like some bundle of damp washing slowly falling. Her eyes drooped, heavy bags held the tiredness under them.

To her surprise, there was a light on in their flat. Then she heard the ticking of the fan. She had forgotten to turn it off when they went up to the terrace and it seemed the electricity had been switched on again, earlier than they had expected. The relief of it brought her energy back in a bound. She bustled up the stairs. I'll bring him down – he'll get some hours of sleep after all, she told herself.

'It's all right,' she called out as she went up to the terrace 57 again. 'That electricity is on again. Come, I'll help you down – you'll get some sleep in your own bed after all.'

'Leave me alone,' he replied, quite gently.

'Why? Why?' she cried. 'I'll help you. You can get into your own bed, you'll be quite comfortable –'

'Leave me alone,' he said again in that still voice. 'It is cool now.'

It was. Morning had stirred up some breeze off the sluggish river Jumma beneath the city walls, and it was carried over the rooftops of the stifled city, pale and fresh and delicate. It brought with it the morning light, as delicate and sweet as the breeze itself, a pure pallor unlike the livid glow of artificial lights. This lifted higher and higher into the dome of the sky, diluting the darkness there till it, too, grew pale and gradually shades of blue and mauve tinted it lightly.

The old man lay flat and still, gazing up, his mouth hanging open as if to let it pour into him, as cool and fresh as water.

Then, with a swirl and flutter of feathers, a flock of pigeons hurtled upwards and spread out against the dome of the sky – opalescent, sunlit, like small pearls. They caught the light as they rose, turned brighter till they turned at last into crystals, into prisms of light. Then they disappeared into the soft, deep blue of the morning.

A Note on Anita Desai

Anita Desai 1937— Indian novelist, born in Mussoorie. A very polished writer, she describes surface realities sharply, but uses them also as markers for her characters' interior lives; indeed, *The Village by the Sea* (1982), though intended for children, achieves social commitment simply through the great clarity of its scenes of poverty. *Cry, the Peacock* (1963) and *Voices in the City* (1965) feature sensitive Hindu women of orthodox background seeking unorthodox means of fulfilment that lead to despair and insanity. In *Bye-Bye, Blackbird* (1971) two Indians in England gradually understand their relationship with India. The claustrophobia of family-bound women is explored in *Where Shall We Go This Summer?* (1975) and *Fire on the Mountain* (1977). Particularly distinguished is *Clear Light of Day* (1980), about an embittered woman discovering her own human shortcomings. *In Custody* (1984), her first novel centred on a male character, is convoluted in style and thematically hazy.